A Thorny P

Volume 02

Georg Ebers

(Translator: Clara Bell)

Alpha Editions

This edition published in 2023

ISBN : 9789357948425

Design and Setting By
Alpha Editions
www.alphaedis.com
Email - info@alphaedis.com

Contents

VOLUME 2.

CHAPTER V.

The crowds on the road were now homeward bound, and they were all in such wild, high spirits that, from what was to be seen and heard, it could never have been supposed that they had come from so mournful a scene. They took the road by the sea leading from the Nekropolis to Eleusis, wandering on in the glowing moonlight.

A great procession of Greeks had been to Eleusis, to celebrate the mysteries after the manner of the Greek Eleusis, on which that of Alexandria was modeled. The newly initiated, and the elder adepts, whose duty it was to superintend their reception, had remained in the temple; but the other mystics now swelled the train of those who were coming from the city of the dead.

Here, indeed, Serapis took the place of Pluto, and much that was Greek had assumed strange and Egyptian forms: even the order of the ceremonies had been entirely changed; still, on the African, as on the Attic shore, the Greek cry went up, "To the sea, O mystics!" and the bidding to Iakchos: "Be with us, O Iakchos!"

It could be heard from afar, but the voices of the shouters were already weary, and most of the torches had burned low. The wreaths of ivy and myrtle in their hair were limp; the singers of the hymn no longer kept their ranks; and even Iambe, whose jests had cheered the mourning Demeter, and whose lips at Eleusis had overflowed with witticisms, was exhausted and silent. She still held in her hand the jar from which she had given the bereaved goddess a reviving draught, but it was empty and she longed for a drink. She was indeed a he: for it was a youth in woman's dress who played the rollicking part of Iambe, and it was Alexander's friend and comrade Diodoros who had represented the daughter of Pan and Echo, who, the legend said, had acted as slave in the house of Metaneira, the Eleusinian queen, when Demeter took refuge there. His sturdy legs had good reason to be as weary as his tongue, which had known no rest for five hours.

But he caught sight of the large vehicle drawn by four horses, in which the vast corn-measure, the kalathos, which Serapis wore as his distinguishing head-gear, had been conveyed to Eleusis. It was empty now, for the contents had been offered to the god, and the four black horses had an easy task with the great wagon. No one had as yet thought of using it as a conveyance back to the town; but Diodoros, who was both ingenious and tired, ran after it and leaped up. Several now wanted to follow his example, but he pushed them off, even thrusting at them with a newly lighted torch, for he could not be quiet in spite of his fatigue. In the midst of the skirmishing he perceived his friend and Melissa.

His heart had been given to the gentle girl ever since they had been playmates in his father's garden, and when he saw her, walking along downcast, while her brother sported with his neighbor's daughters, he beckoned to her, and, as she refused to accompany him in the wagon, he nimbly sprang off, lifted her up in his arms, made strong by exercise in the Palaestra, and gently deposited her, in spite of her struggles, on the flat floor of the car, by the side of the empty kalathos.

"The rape of Persephone!" he cried. "The second performance in one. night!"

Then the old reckless spirit seized Alexander too.

With as much gay audacity—as though he were free of every care and grief, and had signed a compact with Fortune, he picked up pretty Ino, lifted her into the wagon, as Diodoros had done with his sister, and exclaiming, "The third performance!" seated himself by her side.

His bold example found immediate imitators. "A fourth!" "A fifth!" cried one and another, shouting and laughing, with loud calls on Iakchos.

The horses found it hard work, for all along the edge of the car, and round the kalathos of the great Serapis, sat the merry young couples in close array. Alexander and Melissa soon were wreathed with myrtle and ivy. In the vehicle and among the crowd there were none but radiant and frolicsome faces, and no sound but triumphant revelry.

Fatigue was forgotten; it might have been supposed that the sinister sisters, Care and Sorrow, had been banished from earth.

There was a smile even on Melissa's sweet, calm face. At first her old friend's audacious jest had offended her maidenly coyness; but if Diodoros had always loved her, so had she always loved him; and as other well-conducted girls had been content to have the like done to them, and her companion so confidently and roguishly sued for pardon, she gave him a smile which filled his heart with rapture, and said more than words.

It was a comfort, too, to sit still and rest.

She spoke but little, but even she forgot what troubled her when she felt her friend's hand on hers, and he whispered to her that this was the most delightful night he had ever known, and that, of all the sweets the gods had created, she was to him the sweetest?

The blue sea spread before them, the full moon mirrored on its scarcely heaving surface like a tremulous column of pure and shining silver. The murmur of the ripples came up from the strand as soothing and inviting as the song of the Nereids; and if a white crest of foam rose on a wave, she could fancy it was the arm of Thetis or Galatea. There, where the blue was deepest, the sea-god Glaukos must dwell, and his heart be gladdened by the merry doings on shore.

Nature is so great; and as the thought came to her that her heart was not too small to take its greatness in, even to the farthest horizon, it filled her with glad surprise.

And Nature was bountiful too. Melissa could see the happy and gracious face of a divinity in everything she looked upon. The immortals who had afflicted her, and whom she had often bitterly accused, could be kind and merciful too. The sea, on whose shining surface the blue vault of heaven with the moon and stars rocked and twinkled, the soft breeze which fanned her brow, the new delicious longing which filled her heart-all she felt and was conscious of, was a divinity or an emanation of the divine. Mighty Poseidon and majestic Zeus, gentle Selene, and the sportive children of the god of winds, seemed to be strangely near her as she rode along. And it was the omnipotent son of Kypris, no doubt, who stirred her heart to beat higher than it had ever done before.

Her visit to her mother's grave, too, her prayer and her offerings there, had perhaps moved the spirit of the beloved dead to hover near her now as a guardian genius.

Still, now and again the memory of something terrible passed over her soul like a sweeping shadow; but what it was which threatened her and those dear to her she did not see, and would not now inquire. What the morrow might bring should not cloud the enchantment of this hour. For oh, how fair the world was, and how blessed might mortals be!

"Iakchos! Iakchos!" the voices about her shouted, and it sounded as gleeful as though the breasts of the revelers were overflowing with gladness; and as the scented curls of Diodoros bent over her head, as his hand closed on hers, and his whispered words of love were in her ear, she murmured: "Alexander is right; the world is a banqueting-hall, and life is fair."

"So fair!" echoed the youth, pensively. Then he shouted aloud to his companions: "The world is a banqueting-hall! Bring roses, bring wine, that we may sacrifice to Eros, and pour libations to Dionysus. Light the flaming torches! Iakchos! come, Iakchos, and sanctify our glad festival!"

"Come, Iakchos, come!" cried one and another, and soon the enthusiastic youth's cry was taken up on all sides. But wine-skin and jar were long since emptied.

Hard by, below the cliff, and close to the sea, was a tavern, at the sign of the Cock. Here cool drink was to be had; here the horses might rest- for the drivers had been grumbling bitterly at the heavy load added to the car over the deep sand—and here there was a level plot, under the shade of a spreading sycamore, which had often before now served as a floor for the choric dance.

The vehicle soon drew up in front of the whitewashed inn, surrounded on three sides by a trellised arbor, overgrown with figs and vine. The young couples sprang to the ground; and, while the host and his slave dragged up a huge wine-jar with two ears, full of the red juice of the grape, fresh torches were lighted and stuck on poles or fastened to the branches of the sycamore, the youths took their places eager for the dance, and suddenly the festal song went up from their clear throats unbidden, and as though inspired by some mysterious power:

> Iakchos, come! oh, come, Iakchos!
> Hither come, to the scene of our revel,
> The gladsome band of the faithful.
> Shake the fragrant, berried garland,
> Myrtle-twined, that crowns thy love-locks,
> Shedding its odors!
> Tread the measure, with fearless stamp,
> Of this our reckless, rapturous dance,
> In holy rejoicing!
> Hand in hand, thrice beatified,
> Lo we thread the rhythmic, fanciful,
> Mystical mazes!

And the dance begins. Youths and maidens advance to meet each other with graceful movements. Every step must be a thing of beauty, every bend and rising, while the double flutes play faster and faster, and the measured rhythm becomes a wild whirl. They all know the dance, and the music is a guide to the feeling to be expressed; the dancing must be suited to it. Every gesture is a stroke of color which may beautify or mar the picture. Body and spirit are in perfect harmony, combining to represent the feelings that stir the soul. It is a work of art, the art of the arms and feet. Even when passion is at the highest the guiding law is observed. Nay, when the dancers fly wildly apart, they, not merely come together again with unerring certainty, but form in new combination another delightful and perfectly harmonious picture.

"Seek and find" this dance might be called, for the first idea is to represent the wandering of Demeter in search of her daughter Persephone, whom Pluto has carried off to the nether world, till she finds her and clasps her in her motherly arms once more. Thus does the earth bewail the reaped fruit of the field, which is buried in the ground in the winter sowing, to rise again in the spring; thus does a faithful heart pine during absence till it is reunited to the beloved one; thus do we mourn our dead till our soul is assured of their resurrection: and this belief is the end and clew to the mystery.

All this grief and search, this longing and crying for the absent, this final restoration and the bliss of new possession, is set forth by the youths and damsels-now in slow and now in vehement action, but always with infinite grace.

Melissa threw her whole soul into the dance while Demeter was seeking the lost Persephone, her thoughts were with her brothers; and she laughed as heartily as any one at the jests with which Iambe cheered the stricken mother. And when the joy of meeting was to find expression, she need not think of anything but the fact that the youth who held out his hand to her loved her and cared for her. In this, for the moment, lay the end of all her longing and seeking, the fulfillment of every wish; and as the chorus shouted, "Iakchos!" again and again, her soul seemed to have taken wings.

The reserve of her calm and maidenly nature broke down; in her ecstasy she snatched from her shoulder the wreath of ivy with which Diodoros had decked her, and waved it aloft. Her long hair had fallen loose in the dance and flowed wildly about her, and her shout of "Iakchos!" rang clear in the night air.

The youth she loved gazed at her with ravished eyes, as at some miracle; she, heedless of the others, threw her arms round his neck, and, as he kissed her, she said once more, but loud enough now to be heard from afar, "The world is a banqueting-hall!" and again she joined in the shout of "Iakchos!" her eyes bright with excitement. Cups filled high with wine now circulated among the mad-cap mystics; even Melissa refreshed herself, handing the beaker to her lover, and Diodoros raised to his mouth that place on the rim which her lips had touched.

"O life! fount of joys!" cried Diodoros, kissing her and pressing her closer to him. "Come, Iakchos! Behold with envy how thankfully two mortals can bless the gift of life. But where is Alexander? To none but to our Andreas have I ever confided the secret I have borne in my heart since that day when we went to the circus. But now! Oh, it is so much happiness for two hearts! My friend, too, must have part in it!"

At this Melissa clasped her hand to her brow, as though waking from a dream. How hot she was from dancing, and the unusual strength of the wine and water she had drunk!

The danger impending over both her brothers came back to her mind. She had always been accustomed to think of others rather than herself, and her festal mood dropped from her suddenly, like a mantle of which the brooch breaks. She vehemently shook herself free of her lover's embrace, and her eyes glanced from one to another in rapid search.

There stood pretty Ino, who had danced the mazy measure with Alexander. Panting for breath, she stood leaning her weary head and tangled hair against the trunk of the tree, a wine-cup upside down in her right hand. It must be empty; but where was he who had emptied it?

Her neighbor's daughter would surely know. Had the reckless youth quarreled with the girl? No, no!

One of the tavern-keeper's slaves, Ino told her, had whispered something to Alexander, whereupon he had instantly followed the man into the house. Melissa knew that it could be no trivial matter which detained him there, and hurried after him into the tavern.

The host, a Greek, and his buxom wife, affected not to know for whom she was inquiring; but, perceiving the anxiety which spoke in every line of the girl's face, when she explained that she was Alexander's sister, they at first looked at each other doubtingly, and then the woman, who had children of her own, who fondly loved each other, felt her heart swell within her, and she whispered, with her finger on her lips: "Do not be uneasy, pretty maid; my husband will see him well through."

And then Melissa heard that the Egyptian, who had alarmed her in the Nekropolis, was the spy Zminis, who, as her old slave Dido had once told her, had been a rejected suitor of her mother's before she had married Heron, and who was therefore always glad to bring trouble on all who belonged to her father's house. How often had she heard of the annoyances in which this man had involved her father and Alexander, who were apt to be very short with the man!

This tale-bearer, who held the highest position as guardian of the peace under the captain of the night-watch, was of all men in the city the most hated and feared; and he had heard her brother speaking of Caesar in a tone of mockery which was enough to bring him to prison, to the quarries, nay, to death. Glaukias, the sculptor, had previously seen the Egyptian on the bridge, where he had detained those who were returning home from the city of the dead. He and his followers had already stopped the poet Argeios on his way, but the thyrsus staves of the Dionysiac revelers had somewhat spoiled the game for him and his satellites. He was probably still standing on the bridge. Glaukias had immediately run back, at any risk, to warn Alexander. He and the painter were now in hiding, and would remain in safety, come what might, in the cellar at the Cock, till the coast was clear again. The tavern-keeper strongly advised no one to go meddling with his wine-skins and jars.

"Much less that Egyptian dog!" cried his wife, doubling her fist as though the hated mischief-maker stood before her already.

"Poor, helpless lamb!" she murmured to herself, as she looked compasionately at the fragile, town-bred girl, who stood gazing at the ground as if she had been struck by lightning. She remembered, too, how hard life had seemed to her in her own young days, and glanced with pride at her brawny arms, which were able indeed to work and manage.

But what now?

The drooping flower suddenly raised her head, as if moved by a spring, exclaiming: "Thank you heartily, thank you! But that will never do. If Zminis searches your premises he will certainly go into the cellar; for what can he not do in Caesar's name? I will not part from my brother."

"Then you, too, are a welcome guest at the Cock," interrupted the woman, and her husband bowed low, assuring her that the Cock was as much her house as it was his.

But the helpless town-bred damsel declined this friendly invitation; for her shrewd little head had devised another plan for saving her brother, though the tavern-keepers, to whom she confided it in a whisper, laughed and shook their heads over it. Diodoros was waiting outside in anxious impatience; he loved her, and he was her brother's best friend. All that he could do to save Alexander he would gladly do, she knew. On the estate which would some day be his, there was room and to spare to hide the fugitives, for one of the largest gardens in the town was owned by his father. His extensive grounds had been familiar to her from her childhood, for her own mother and her lover's had been friends; and Andreas, the freedman, the overseer of Polybius's gardens and plantations, was dearer to her and her brothers than any one else in Alexandria.

Nor had she deceived herself, for Diodoros made Alexander's cause his own, in his eager, vehement way; and the plan for his deliverance seemed doubly admirable as proceeding from Melissa. In a few minutes Alexander and the sculptor were released from their hiding-place, and all further care for them was left to Diodoros.

They were both very, craftily disguised. No one would have recognized the artists in two sailors, whose Phrygian caps completely hid their hair, while a heavy fisherman's apron was girt about their loins; still less would any one have suspected from their laughing faces that imprisonment, if nothing worse, hung over them. Their change of garb had given rise to so much fun; and now, on hearing how they were to be smuggled into the town, their merriment grew higher, and proved catching to those who were taken into the secret. Only Melissa was oppressed with anxious care, in spite of her lover's eager consolation.

Glaukias, a man of scarcely middle height, was sure of not being recognized, and he and his comrades looked forward to whatever might happen as merely an amusing jest. At the same time they had to balk the hated chief of the city guards and his menials of their immediate prey; but they had played them a trick or two ere now. It might turn out really badly for Alexander; still, it was only needful to keep him concealed till Caesar should arrive; then he would be safe, for the Emperor would certainly absorb all the thoughts and time of the captain of the night-watch and his chief officers. In Alexandria, anything once past was so soon forgotten! When once Caracalla was gone—and it was to be hoped that he would not stay long—no one would ever think again of any biting speech made before his arrival.

The morning must bring what it might, so long as the present moment was gay!

So, refreshed and cheered by rest and wine, the party of mystics prepared to set out again; and, as the procession started, no one who did not know it had observed that the two artists, disguised as sailors, were, by Melissa's advice, hidden inside the kalathos of Serapis, which would easily have held six, and was breast-high even for Alexander, who was a tall man. They squatted on the floor of the huge vessel, with a jar of wine between them, and peeped over now and then with a laugh at the girls, who had again seated themselves on the edge of the car.

When they were fairly on their way once more, Alexander and his companions were so daring that, whenever they could do it unobserved, they pelted the damsels with the remains of the corn, or sprinkled them with wine-drops. Glaukias had the art of imitating the pattering of rain and the humming of a fly to perfection with his lips; and when the girls complained of the tiresome insect buzzing in their faces, or declared, when a drop fell on them, that in spite of the blue and cloudless sky it was certainly beginning to rain, the two men had to cover their mouths with their hands, that their laughter might not betray them.

Melissa, who had comforted Ino with the assurance that Alexander had been called away quite unexpectedly, was now sitting by her side, and perceived, of course, what tricks the men in the kalathos were playing; but, instead of amusing her, they only made her anxious.

Every one about her was laughing and joking, but for her all mirth was at an end. Fear, indeed, weighed on her like an incubus, when the car reached the bridge and rattled across it. It was lined with soldiers and lictors, who looked closely at each one, even at Melissa herself. But no one spoke to her, and when the water lay behind them she breathed more freely. But only for a moment; for she suddenly remembered that they would presently have to pass through the gate leading past Hadrian's western wall into the town. If Zminis were waiting there instead of on the bridge, and were to search the vehicle, then all would be lost, for he had looked her, too, in the face with those strange, fixed eyes of his; and that where he saw the sister he would also seek the brother, seemed to her quite certain. Thus her presence was a source of peril to Alexander, and she must at any cost avert that.

She immediately put out her hand to Diodoros, who was walking at her side, and with his help slipped down from her seat. Then she whispered her fears to him, and begged him to quit the party and conduct her home.

This was a surprising and delightful task for her lover. With a jesting word he leaped on to the car, and even succeeded in murmuring to Alexander, unobserved, that Melissa had placed herself under his protection. When they got home, they could tell Heron and Andreas that the youths were safe in hiding. Melissa could explain, to-morrow morning, how everything had happened. Then he drew Melissa's arm through his, loudly shouted, "Iakchos!" and with a swift dance-step soon outstripped the wagon.

Not fifty paces beyond, large pine torches sent bright flames up skyward, and by their light the girl could see the dreaded gateway, with the statues of Hadrian and Sabina, and in front of them, in the middle of the road, a horseman, who, as they approached, came trotting forward to meet them on his tall steed. His head towered above every one else in the road; and as she looked up at him her heart almost ceased beating, for her eyes met those of the dreaded Egyptian; their white balls showed plainly in his brown, lean face, and their cruel, evil sparkle had stamped them clearly on her memory.

On her right a street turned off from the road, and saying in a low tone, "This way," she led Diodoros, to his surprise, into the shadow. His heart beat high. Did she, whose coy and maidenly austerity before and after the intoxication of the dance had vouchsafed him hardly a kind look or a clasp of the hand-did she even yearn for some tender embrace alone and in darkness? Did the quiet, modest girl, who, since she had ceased to be a child, had but rarely given him a few poor words, long to tell him that which hitherto only her bright eyes and the kiss of her pure young lips had betrayed?

He drew her more closely to him in blissful expectation; but she shyly shrank from his touch, and before he could murmur a single word of love she exclaimed in terror, as though the hand of the persecutor were already laid on her: "Fly, fly! That house will give us shelter."

And she dragged him after her into the open doorway of a large building. Scarcely had they entered the dark vestibule when the sound of hoofs was heard, and the glare of torches dispelled the darkness outside.

"Zminis! It is he—he is following us!" she whispered, scarcely able to speak; and her alarm was well founded, for the Egyptian had recognized her, and supposed her companion to be Alexander. He had ridden down the street with his torchbearers, but where she had hidden herself his keen eyes could not detect, for the departing sound of hoofs betrayed to the breathless listeners that the pursuer had left their hiding-place far behind him. Presently the pavement in front of the house which sheltered them rang again with the tramp of the horse, till it died away at last in the direction of Hadrian's gate. Not till then did Melissa lift her hand from her painfully throbbing heart.

But the Egyptian would, no doubt, have left his spies in the street, and Diodoros went out to see if the road was clear. Melissa remained alone in the dark entrance, and began to be anxious as to how she could explain her presence there if the inhabitants should happen to discover it; for in this vast building, in spite of the lateness of the hour, there still was some one astir. She had for some minutes heard a murmuring sound which reached her from an inner chamber; but it was only by degrees that she collected herself so far as to listen more closely, to ascertain whence it came and what it could mean.

A large number of persons must be assembled there, for she could distinguish several male voices, and now and then a woman's. A door was opened. She shrank closer to the wall, but the seconds became minutes, and no one appeared.

At last she fancied she heard the moving of benches or seats, and many voices together shouting she knew not what. Then again a door creaked on its hinges, and after that all was so still that she could have heard a needle drop on the floor; and this alarming silence continued till presently a deep, resonant man's voice was audible.

The singular manner in which this voice gave every word its full and equal value suggested to her fancy that something was being read aloud. She could distinctly hear the sentence with which the speech or reading began. After a short pause it was repeated somewhat more quickly, as though the speaker had this time uttered it from his own heart.

It consisted of these six simple words, "The fullness of the time was come"; and Melissa listened no more to the discourse which followed, spoken as it was in a low voice, for this sentence rang in her ears as if it were repeated by an echo.

She did not, to be sure, understand its meaning, but she felt as though it must have some deep significance. It came back to her again and again, like a melody which haunts the inward ear against our will; and her meditative fancy was trying to solve its meaning, when Diodoros returned to tell her that the street was quite empty. He knew now where they were, and, if she liked, he could lead her by a way which would not take them through the gate. Only Christians, Egyptians, and other common folks dwelt in this quarter; however, since his duty as her protector had this day begun, he would fulfill it to the best of his ability.

She went with him out into the street, and when they had gone a little way he clasped her to him and kissed her hair.

His heart was full. He knew now that she, whom he had loved when she walked in his father's garden in her little child's tunic, holding her mother's hand, returned his passion. Now the time was come for asking whether she would permit him to beg her father's leave to woo her.

He stopped in the shadow of a house near, and, while he poured out to her all that stirred his breast, carried away by tender passion, and describing in his vehement way how great and deep his love was, in spite of the utter fatigue which weighed on her body and soul after so many agitations, she felt with deep thankfulness the immense happiness of being more precious than aught else on earth to a dear, good man. Love, which had so long lain dormant in her as a bud, and then opened so quickly only to close again under her alarms, unfolded once more and blossomed for him again—not as it had done just now in passionate ecstasy, but, as beseemed her calm, transparent nature, with moderated joy, which, however, did not lack due warmth and winning tenderness.

Happiness beyond words possessed them both. She suffered him to seal his vows with kisses, herself offering him her lips, as her heart swelled with fervent thanksgiving for so much joy and such a full measure of love.

She was indeed a precious jewel, and the passion of his stormy heart was tempered by such genuine reverence that he gladly kept within the bounds which her maidenly modesty prescribed. And how much they had to say to each other in this first opening of their hearts, how many hopes for the future found utterance in words! The minutes flew on and became hours, till at last Melissa begged him to quit the marble seat on which they had so long been resting, if indeed her feet could still carry her home.

Little as it pleased him, he did her bidding. But as they went on he felt that she hung heavy on his arm and could only lift her little feet with the greatest difficulty. The street was too dark for him to see how pale she was; and yet he never took his eyes off her dear but scarcely distinguishable features. Suddenly he heard a faint whisper as in a dream, "I can go no farther," and at once led her back to the marble seat.

He first carefully spread his mantle over the stone and then wrapped her in it as tenderly as a mother might cover her shivering child, for a cooler breeze gave warning of the coming dawn. He himself crept close under the wall by her side, so as not to be seen, for a long train of people, with servants carrying lanterns before them, now came out of the house they had just left and down the street. Who these could be who walked at so late an hour in such solemn silence neither of them knew. They certainly sent up no joyful shout of "Iakchos!" no wild lament; no cheerful laughter nor sounds of mourning were to be heard from the long procession which passed along the street, two and two, at a slow pace. As soon as they had passed the last houses, men and women alike began to sing; no leader started them, nor lyre accompanied them, and yet their song went up as though with one voice.

Diodoros and Melissa knew every note sung by the Greeks or Egyptians of Alexandria, at this or any other festival, but this melody was strange to them; and when the young man whispered to the girl, "What is it that they are singing?" she replied, as though startled from sleep, "They are no mere mortals!"

Diodoros shuddered; he fancied that the procession was floating above the earth; that, if they had been indeed men of flesh and blood, their steps would have been more distinctly audible on the pavement. Some of them appeared to him to be taller than common mortals, and their chant was certainly that of another world than this where he dwelt. Perhaps these were daimons, the souls of departed Egyptians, who, after a midnight visit to those they had left behind them, were returning to the rock tombs, of which there were many in the stony hills to which this street led. They were walking toward these tombs, and not toward the gate; and Diodoros whispered his suspicion to his companion, clasping his hand on an amulet in the semblance of an eye, which his Egyptian nurse had fastened round his neck long ago with an Anubic thread, to protect him against the evil-eye and magic spells.

But Melissa was listening with such devout attention to the chant that she did not hear him. The fatigue which had reached such a painful climax had, during this peaceful rest, given way to a blissful unconsciousness of self. It was a kind of happiness to feel no longer the burden of exhaustion, and the song of the wanderers was like a cradle-song, lulling her to sweet dreams. It filled her with gladness, and yet it was not glad, not even cheerful. It went to her heart, and yet it was not mournful-not in the least like the passionate lament of Isis for Osiris, or that of Demeter bewailing her daughter. The emotion it aroused in her was a sweetly sorrowful compassion, which included herself, her brothers, her father, her lover, all who were doomed to suffering and death, even the utter stranger, for whom she had hitherto felt no sympathy.

And the compassion bore within it a sense of comfort which she could not explain, or perhaps would not inquire into. It struck her, too, now and then, that the strain had a ring as of thanksgiving. It was, no doubt, addressed to the gods, and for that reason it appealed to her, and she would gladly have joined in it, for she, too, was grateful to the immortals, and above all to Eros, for the love which had been born in her heart and had found such an ardent return. She sighed as she listened to every note of the chant, and it worked upon her like a healing draught.

The struggle of her will against bodily fatigue, and finally against the mental exhaustion of so much bliss, the conviction that her heavy, weary feet would perhaps fail to carry her home, and that she must seek shelter somewhere for the night, had disturbed her greatly. Now she was quite calm, and as much at ease as she was at home sitting with her father, her stitching in her hand, while she dreamed of her mother and her childhood in the past. The singing had fallen on her agitated soul like the oil poured by the mariner on the sea to still the foaming breakers. She felt it so.

She could not help thinking of the time when she could fall asleep on her mother's bosom in the certainty that tender love was watching over her. The happiness of childhood, when she loved everything she knew-her family, the slaves, her father's birds, the flowers in the little garden, the altar of the goddess to whom she made offering, the very stars in the sky-seemed to come over her, and there she sat in dreamy lassitude, her head on her lover's shoulder, till the last stragglers of the procession, who, were women, many of them carrying little lamps in their hands, had almost all gone past.

Then she suddenly felt an eager jerk in the shoulder on which her head was resting.

"Look—look there!" he whispered; and as her eyes followed the direction of his finger, she too started, and exclaimed, "Korinna!—Did you know her?"

"She had often come to my father's garden," he replied, "and I saw her portrait in Alexander's room. These are souls from Hades that we have seen. We must offer sacrifice, for those to whom they show themselves they draw after them." At this Melissa, too, shuddered, and exclaimed in horror: "O Diodoros, not to death! We will ask the priests to-morrow morning what sacrifice may redeem us. Anything rather than the grave and the darkness of Hades!—Come, I am strong again now. Let us get away from hence and go home."

"But we must go through the gate now," replied the youth. "It is not well to follow in the footsteps of the dead."

Melissa, however, insisted on going on through the street. Terrified as she was of the nether world and the disembodied souls, she would on no account risk falling into the hands of the horrible Egyptian, who might compel her to betray her brother's hiding-place; and Diodoros, who was ashamed to show her the fears which still possessed him, did as she desired.

But it was a comfort to him in this horror of death, which had come over him now for the first time in his life, to kiss the maid once more, and hold her warm hand in his as they walked on; while the strange chant of the nocturnal procession still rang in her ears, and now and then the words recurred to her mind which she had heard in the house where the departed souls had gathered together:

"The fullness of the time was come."

Did this refer to the hour when the dead came to the end of their life on earth; or was there some great event impending on the city and its inhabitants, for which the time had now come? Had the words anything to do with Caesar's visit? Had the dead come back to life to witness the scenes which they saw approaching with eyes clearer than those of mortals?

And then she remembered Korinna, whose fair, pale face had been strangely lighted up by the lamp she carried; and, again, the Magian's assurance that the souls of the departed were endowed with every faculty possessed by the living, and that "those who knew" could see them and converse with them.

Then Serapion had been right in saying this; and her hand trembled in her lover's as she thought to herself that the danger which now threatened Philip was estrangement from the living through intercourse with the dead. Her own dead mother, perhaps, had floated past among these wandering souls, and she grieved to think that she had neglected to look for her and give her a loving greeting. Even Diodoros, who was not generally given to silent meditation, had his own thoughts to pursue; and so they walked on in silence till suddenly they heard a dull murmur of voices. This startled them, and looking up they saw before them the rocky cliffs in which the Egyptians long since, and now in later times the Christians, had hewn caves and tombs. From the door of one of these, only a few paces beyond where they stood, light streamed out; and as they were about to pass it a large dog barked. Immediately on this a man came out, and in a rough, deep voice asked them the pass-word. Diodoros, seized with sudden terror of the dark figure, which he believed to be a risen ghost, took to his heels, dragging Melissa with him. The dog flew after them, barking loudly; and when the youth stooped to pick up a stone to scare him off, the angry brute sprang on him and dragged him down.

Melissa screamed for help, but the gruff voice angrily bade her be silent. Far from obeying him, the girl shouted louder than ever; and now, out of the entrance to the cave, close behind the scene of the disaster, came a number of men with lamps and tapers. They were the same daimons whose song she had heard in the street; she could not be mistaken. On her knees, by the side of her lover as he lay on the ground, she stared up at the apparitions. A stone flew at the dog to scare him off, and a second, larger than the first, whisked past her and hit Diodoros on the head; she heard the dull blow. At this a cold hand seemed to clutch her heart; everything about her melted into one whirling, colorless cloud. Pale as death, she threw up her arms to protect herself, and then, overcome with terror and fatigue, with a faint cry of anguish she lost consciousness.

When she opened her eyes again her head was resting in the lap of a kind, motherly woman, while some men were just bearing away the senseless form of Diodoros on a bier.

CHAPTER VI.

The sun had risen an hour since. Heron had betaken himself to his workshop, whistling as he went, and in the kitchen his old slave Argutis was standing over the hearth preparing his master's morning meal. He dropped a pinch of dill into the barley-porridge, and shook his gray head solemnly.

His companion Dido, a Syrian, whose wavy white hair contrasted strangely with her dark skin, presently came in, and, starting up, he hastily inquired, "Not in yet?"

"No," said the other woman, whose eyes were full of tears. "And you know what my dream was. Some evil has come to her, I am certain; and when the master hears of it—" Here she sobbed aloud; but the slave reproved her for useless weeping.

"You never carried her in your arms," whimpered the woman.

"But often enough on my shoulder," retorted the Gaul, for Argutis was a native of Augusta Trevirorum, on the Moselle. "Assoon as the porridge is ready you must take it in and prepare the master."

"That his first fury may fall on me!" said the old woman, peevishly. "I little thought when I was young!"

"That is a very old story," said Argutis, "and we both know what the master's temper is. I should have been off long ago if only you could make his porridge to his mind. As soon as I have dished it I will go to seek Alexander—there is nothing to prevent me—for it was with him that she left the house."

At this the old woman dried her tears, and cried "Yes, only go, and make haste. I will do everything else. Great gods, if she should be brought home dead! I know how it is; she could bear the old man's temper and this moping life no longer, and has thrown herself into the water.

"My dream, my dream! Here—here is the dish, and now go and find the boy. Still, Philip is the elder."

"He!" exclaimed the slave in a scornful tone. "Yes, if you want to know what the flies are talking about! Alexander for me. He has his head screwed on the right way, and he will find her if any man in Egypt can, and bring her back, alive or dead."

"Dead!" echoed Dido, with a fresh burst of sobs, and her tears fell in the porridge, which Argutis, indeed, in his distress of mind had forgotten to salt.

While this conversation was going on the gemcutter was feeding his birds. Can this man, who stands there like any girl, tempting his favorites to feed, with fond words and whistling, and the offer of attractive dainties, be the stormy blusterer of last night? There is not a coaxing name that he does not lavish on them, while he fills their cups with fresh seed and water; and how carefully he moves his big hand as he strews the little cages with clean sand! He would not for worlds scare the poor little prisoners who cheer his lonely hours, and who have long since ceased to fear him. A turtle-dove takes peas, and a hedge-sparrow picks ants' eggs from his lips; a white-throat perches on his left hand to snatch a caterpillar from his right. The huge man was in his garden soon after sunrise gathering the dewy leaves for his feathered pets. But he talks and plays longest with the starling which his lost wife gave him. She had bought it in secret from the Bedouin who for many years had brought shells for sale from the Red Sea, to surprise her husband with the gift. The clever bird had first learned to call her name, Olympias; and then, without any teaching, had picked up his master's favorite lament, "My strength, my strength!"

Heron regarded this bird as a friend who understood him, and, like him, remembered the never-to-be-forsaken dead. For three years had the gem cutter been a widower, and he still thought more constantly and fondly of his lost wife than of the children she had left him. Heron scratched the bird's knowing little head, saying in a tone which betrayed his pity both for himself and his pet "Yes, old fellow, you would rather have a soft white finger to stroke you down. I can hear her now, when she would call you 'sweet little pet,' or 'dear little creature.' We shall neither of us ever hear such gentle, loving words again. Do you remember how she would look up with her dear sweet face—and was it not a lovely face?—when you called her by her name 'Olympias'? How many a time have her rosy lips blown up your feathers, and cried, 'Well done, little fellow! '—Ay, and she would say 'Well done' to me too, when I had finished a piece of work well. Ah, and what an eye she had, particularly for art! But now well, the children give me a good word too, now that her lips are silent!"

"Olympias!" cried the bird loudly and articulately, and the clouds that shadowed the gem-cutter's brow lifted a little, as with an affectionate smile he went on:

"Yes, yes; you would be glad, too, to have her back again. You call her now, as I did yesterday, standing by her grave—and she sends you her love.

"Do you hear, little one? Peck away at the old man's finger; he knows you mean it kindly, and it does not hurt. I was all alone out there, and Selene looked down on us in silence. There was rioting and shouting all round, but I could hear the voice of our dead. She was very near me, and her sad soul showed me that she still cared for me. I had taken a jar of our best wine of Byblos under my cloak; as soon as I had poured oil on her gravestone and shed some of the noble liquor, the earth drank it up as though it were thirsty.

Not a drop was left. Yes, little fellow, she accepted the gift; and when I fell on my knees to meditate on her, she vouchsafed replies to many of my questions.

"We talked together as we used—you know. And we remembered you, too; I gave you her love.

"You understand me, little fellow, don't you? And, I tell you, better times are coming now."

He turned from the bird with a sharp movement of annoyance, for the slave-woman came in with the bowl of barley-porridge.

"You!" exclaimed Heron, in surprise. "Where is Melissa?"

"She will come presently," said the old woman, in a low and doubtful tone.

"Oh, thanks for the oracle!" said the artist, ironically.

"How you mock at a body!" said the old woman. "I meant—But eat first — eat. Anger and grief are ill food for an empty stomach."

Heron sat down to the table and began to eat his porridge, but he presently tossed away the spoon, exclaiming:

"I do not fancy it, eating by myself."

Then, with a puzzled glance at Dido, he asked in a tone of vexation:

"Well, why are you waiting here? And what is the meaning of all that nipping and tugging at your dress? Have you broken another dish? No? Then have done with that cursed head-shaking, and speak out at once!"

"Eat, eat," repeated Dido, retreating to the door, but Heron called her back with vehement abuse; but when she began again her usual complaint, "I never thought, when I was young—" Heron recovered the good temper he had been rejoicing in so lately, and retorted: "Oh! yes, I know, I have the daughter of a great potentate to wait on me. And if it had only occurred to Caesar, when he was in Syria, to marry your sister, I should have had his sister-in-law in my service. But at any rate I forbid howling. You might have learned in the course of thirty years, that I do not eat my fellow-creatures. So, now, confess at once what is wrong in the kitchen, and then go and fetch Melissa." The woman was, perhaps, wise to defer the evil moment as long as possible. Matters might soon change for the better, and good or evil could come only from without. So Dido clung to the literal sense of her master's question, and something note-worthy had actually happened in the kitchen. She drew a deep breath, and told him that a subordinate of the night-watch had come in and asked whether Alexander were in the house, and where his painting-room was.

"And you gave him an exact description?" asked Heron.

But the slave shook her head; she again began to fidget with her dress, and said, timidly:

"Argutis was there, and he says no good can come of the night-watch. He told the man what he thought fit, and sent him about his business."

At this Heron interrupted the old woman with such a mighty blow of his fist on the table that the porridge jumped in the bowl, and he exclaimed in a fury:

"That is what comes of treating slaves as our equals! They begin to think for themselves. A stupid blunder can spoil the best day! The captain of the night-watch, I would have you to know, is a very great man, and very likely a friend of Seleukus's, whose daughter Alexander has just painted. The picture is attracting some attention.—Attention? What am I saying? Every one who has been allowed to see it is quite crazy about it. Everything else that was on show in the embalmers' hall was mere trash by comparison. Often enough have I grumbled at the boy, who would rather be anywhere than here; but, this time, I had some ground for being proud to be his father! And now the captain of the watch sends his secretary, or something of the kind, no doubt, in order to have his portrait, or his wife's or daughter's—if he has one— painted by the artist who did Korinna's; and his own father's slave—it drives me mad to think of it—makes a face at the messenger and sends him all astray. I will give Argutis a lesson! But by this time, perhaps—Just go and fetch him in." With these words Heron again dropped his spoon, wiped his beard, and then, seeing that Dido was still standing before him as though spellbound, twitching her slave's gray gown, he repeated his order in such angry tones—though before he had spoken to her as gently as if she were one of his own children—that the old woman started violently and made for the door, crouching low and whimpering bitterly.

The soft-hearted tyrant was really sorry for the faithful old servant he had bought a generation since for the home to which he had brought his fair young wife, and he began to speak kindly to her, as he had previously done to the birds.

This comforted the old woman so much that again she could not help crying; but, notwithstanding the sincerity of her tears, being accustomed of old to take advantage of her master's moods, she felt that now was the time to tell her melancholy story. First of all she would at any rate see whether Melissa had not meanwhile returned; so she humbly kissed the hem of his robe and hurried away.

"Send Argutis to me!" Heron roared after her, and he returned to his breakfast with renewed energy.

He thought, as he ate, of his son's beautiful work, and the foolish self-importance of Argutis, so faithful, and usually, it must be owned, so shrewd. Then his eyes fell on Melissa's vacant place opposite to him, and he suddenly pushed away his bowl and rose to seek his daughter.

At this moment the starling called, in a clear, inviting tone, "Olympias!" and this cheered him, reminding him of the happy hour he had passed at his wife's grave and the good augury he had had there. The belief in a better time at hand, of which he had spoken to the bird, again took possession of his sanguine soul; and, fully persuaded that Melissa was detained in her own room or elsewhere by some trifling matter, he went to the window and shouted her name; for hers, too, opened on to the garden.

And it seemed as though the dear, obedient girl had come at his bidding, for, as he turned back into the room again, Melissa was standing in the open door.

After the pretty Greek greeting, "Joy be with you," which she faintly answered, he asked her, as fractiously as though he had spent hours of anxiety, where she had been so long. But he was suddenly silent, for he was astonished to see that she had not come from her room, but, as her dress betrayed, from some long expedition. Her appearance, too, had none of the exquisite neatness which it usually displayed; and then—what a state she was in! Whence had she come so early in the day?

The girl took off the kerchief that covered her head, and with a faint groan pushed her tangled hair off her temples, and her bosom heaved as she panted out in a weary voice: "Here I am! But O, father, what a night I have spent!"

Heron could not for a minute or two find words to answer her.

What had happened to the girl? What could it be which made her seem so strange and unlike her self? He gazed at her, speechless, and alarmed by a hundred fearful suspicions. He felt as a mother might who has kissed her child's fresh, healthy lips at night, and in the morning finds them burning with fever.

Melissa had never been ill from the day of her birth; since she had donned the dress of a full-grown maiden she had never altered; day after day and at all hours she had been the same in her quiet, useful, patient way, always thinking of her brothers, and caring for him rather than for herself.

It had never entered into his head to suppose that she could alter; and now, instead of the gentle, contented face with faintly rosy cheeks, he saw a pallid countenance and quivering lips. What mysterious fire had this night kindled in those calm eyes, which Alexander was fond of comparing to those of a gazelle? They were sunk, and the dark shadows that encircled them were a shock to his artistic eye. These were the eyes of a girl who had raved like a maenad the night through. Had she not slept in her quiet little room; had she been rushing with Alexander in the wild Bacchic rout; or had something dreadful happened to his son?

Nothing could have been so great a relief to him as to rave and rage as was his wont, and he felt strongly prompted to do so; but there was something in her which moved him to pity or shyness, he knew not which, and kept him quiet. He silently followed her with his eyes while she folded her mantle and kerchief in her orderly way, and hastily gathered together the stray, curly locks of her hair, smoothed them, and bound them round her head.

Some one, however, must break the silence, and he gave a sigh of relief when the girl came up to him and asked him, in a voice so husky as to give him a fresh shock:

"Is it true that a Scythian, one of the nightwatch, has been here already?"

Then he broke out, and it really did him good to give vent to his repressed feelings in an angry speech:

"There again—the wisdom of slaves! The so-called Scythian brought a message from his master.

"The captain of the night-watch—you will see—wishes to honor Alexander with a commission."

"No, no," interrupted the girl. "They are hunting my brother down. I thank the gods that the Scythian should have come; it shows that Alexander is still free."

The gem-cutter clasped his bushy hair in both hands, for it seemed to him that the room was whirling round. But his old habits still got the better of him; he roared out with all the power of his mighty lungs: "What is that? What do you say? What has Alexander done? Where have you—both of you—been?" With two long strides the angry man came close up to the terrified girl; the birds fluttered in their cages, and the starling repeated his cries in melancholy tones. Heron stood still, pushing his fingers through his thick gray hair, and with a sharp laugh exclaimed: "I came away from her grave full of fresh hopes for better days, and this is how they are fulfilled! I looked for fame, and I find disgrace! And you, hussy! where have you spent this night—where have you come from? I ask you once more!"

He raised his fist and shook it close in front of Melissa's eyes.

She stood before him as pale as death, and with wide-open eyes, from which the heavy tears dropped slowly, one by one, trickling down her cheeks as if they were tired. Heron saw them, and his rage melted. He staggered to a seat like a drunken man, and, hiding his face in his hands, moaned aloud, "Wretch,

wretch that I am!" But his child's soft hand was laid on his head; warm, girlish lips kissed his brow; and Melissa whispered beseechingly: "Peace, father, peace. All may yet be well. I have something to tell you that will make you glad too; yes, I am sure it will make you glad."

Her father shrugged his shoulders incredulously, but wanted to know immediately what the miracle was that could smooth his brow. Melissa, however, would not tell him till it came in its place in her story. So he had to submit; he drew his seat up to the table, and took up a lump of modeling-wax to keep his restless fingers employed while he listened. She, too, sat down; she could scarcely stand.

At first he listened calmly to her narrative; and when she told him of Alexander's jest at Caesar's expense his face brightened. His Alexandrian blood and his relish for a biting speech got the upper hand; he gave a sounding slap on his mighty leg, and exclaimed: "A cursed good thought! But the boy forgot that when Zeus only lamed his son it was because he is immortal; while Caesar's brother was as feeble a mortal as Caracalla himself is said to be at this day."

He laughed noisily; but it was for the last time that morning; for hardly had he heard the name of Zminis, and learned that it was he who had over heard Alexander, than he threw down the wax and started to his feet in horror, crying:

"That dog, who dared to cast his eyes on your mother, and persecuted her long after she had shown him the door! That sly mischief-maker! Many a time has he set snares in our path. If he succeeds in tightening the noose into which the boy has so heedlessly thrust his head—But first tell me, has he caught him already, or is Alexander still at liberty?"

But no one, not even Argutis, who was still out on the search, could tell him this; and he was now so greatly disturbed that, during the rest of Melissa's narrative, he perpetually paced the room, interrupting her now and then with questions or with outbursts of indignation. And then it occurred to him that he ought himself to seek his son, and he occupied himself with getting ready to go out.

Even when she spoke of the Magian, and his conviction that those who know are able to hold intercourse with the souls of the dead, he shrugged his shoulders incredulously, and went on lacing his sandals. But when Melissa assured him that not she alone, but Diodoros with her, had seen the wandering soul of the departed Korinna in the train of ghosts, he dropped the straps he had bound round his ankle, and asked her who this Magian was, and where he might be found. However, she knew no more than that his name was Serapion, and she briefly described his dignified presence.

Heron had already seen the man, and he seemed still to be thinking of him, when Melissa, with a blush and downcast eyes, confessed that, as soon as he was well again, Diodoros was coming to her father to ask her of him in marriage.

It was a long story before she came at last to her own concerns, but it was always her way not to think of herself till every one else had had his due.

But what about her father? Had she spoken inaudibly, or was he really unable to-day to be glad? or what ailed him, that he paid no heed to the news which, even for him, was not without its importance, but, without a word of consent or disapproval, merely bade her go on with her story?

Melissa called him by name, as if to wake a man from sleep, and asked whether it were indeed possible that he really felt no pleasure in the happy prospect that lay before her, and that she had confessed to him. And now Heron lent an ear, and gave her to understand the satisfaction of his fatherly heart by kissing her. This news, in fact, made up for much that was evil, for Diodoros was a son-in-law after his own heart, and not merely because he was rich, or because his mother had been so great a friend of Olympias's. No, the young man's father was, like himself, one of the old Macedonian stock; he had seen his daughter's lover grow to manhood, and there was not in the city a youth he could more heartily welcome. This he freely admitted; he only regretted that when she should set up house with her husband on the other side of the lake, he (Heron) would be left as lonely as a statue on its pedestal. His sons had already begun to avoid him like a leper!

Then, when he heard of what had befallen Diodoros, and Melissa went on to say that the people who had thrown the stone at the dog were Christians, and that they had carried the wounded youth into a large, clean dwelling, where he was being carefully attended when she had left him, Heron broke out into violent abuse. They were unpatriotic worshipers of a crucified Jew, who multiplied like vermin, and only wanted to turn the good old order of things upside down. But this time they should see—the hypocrites, who pretended to so much humanity, and then set ferocious dogs on peaceful folk!—they should learn that they could not fall on a Macedonian citizen without paying for it.

He indignantly refused to hear Melissa's assurance that none of the Christians had set the dog on her lover; she, however, maintained stoutly that it was merely by an unfortunate accident that the stone had hit Diodoros and cut his head so badly. She would not have quitted her lover but that she feared lest her prolonged absence should have alarmed her father.

Heron at last stood still for a minute or two, lost in thought, and then brought out of his chest a casket, from which he took a few engraved gems. He held them carefully up to the light, and asked his daughter: "If I learn from Polybius, to whom I am now going, that they have already caught Alexander, should I venture now, do you think, to offer a couple of choice gems to Titianus, the prefect, to set him free again? He knows what is good, and the captain of the watch is his subordinate."

But Melissa besought him to give up the idea of seeking out Alexander in his hiding-place; for Heron, the gem-cutter, was known to every one, and if a man-at-arms should see him he would certainly follow him. As regarded the prefect, he would not apprehend any one this day, for, as her father knew, Caesar was to arrive at Alexandria at noon, and Titianus must be on the spot to meet him with all his train.

"But if you want to be out of doors and doing," she added, "go to see Philip. Bring him to reason, and discuss with him what is to be done."

She spoke with firm decision, and Heron looked with amazement at the giver of this counsel. Melissa had hitherto cared for his comfort in silence, without expressing any opinions of her own, and submitting to be the lightning-conductor for all his evil tempers. He did not rate her girlish beauty very high, for there were no ugly faces in his family nor in that of his deceased Olympias. And all the other consolations she offered him he took as a matter of course—nay, he sometimes made them a ground of complaint; for he would occasionally fancy that she wanted to assume the place of his beloved lost wife, and he regarded it as a duty to her to show his daughter, and often very harshly and unkindly, how far she was from filling her mother's place.

Thus she had accustomed herself to do her duty as a daughter, with quiet and wordless exactitude, looking for no thanks; while he thought he was doing her a kindness merely by suffering her constant presence. That he should ever exchange ideas with his daughter, or ask her opinion, would have seemed to Heron absolutely impossible; yet it had come to this, and for the second time this morning he looked in her face with utter amazement.

He could not but approve her warning not to betray Alexander's hiding-place, and her suggestion that he should go to see his eldest son coincided with an unspoken desire which had been lurking in his mind ever since she had told him of her having seen a disembodied soul. The possibility of seeing her once more, whose memory was dearer to him than all else on earth, had such a charm, that it moved him more deeply than the danger of his son, who was, nevertheless, very dear to his strangely tempered heart.

So he answered Melissa coolly, as if he were telling her of a decision already formed:

"Of course! I meant to see Philip too; only—" and he paused, for anxiety about Alexander again came to the front—" I can not bear to remain in such uncertainty about the boy."

At this instant the door opened. The new-comer was Andreas, the man to whom Diodoros had advised Alexander to apply for protection and counsel; and Melissa greeted him with filial affection.

He was a freedman in her lover's family, and was the steward and manager of his master's extensive gardens and lands, which were under his absolute control. No one could have imagined that this man had ever been a slave; his face was swarthy, but his fine black eyes lighted it up with a glance of firm self reliance and fiery energy. It was the look of a man who might be the moving spirit of one of those rebellions which were frequent in Alexandria; there was an imperious ring in his voice, and decision in the swift gestures of his hardened but shapely hands.

For twenty years, indeed, he had ruled over the numerous slaves of Polybius, who was an easy-going master, and an invalid from gout in his feet. He was at this time a victim to a fresh attack, and had therefore sent his confidential steward into the town to tell Heron that he approved of his son's choice, and that he would protect Alexander from pursuit.

All this Andreas communicated in few and business-like words; but he then turned to Melissa, and said, in a tone of kindly and affectionate familiarity: "Polybius also wishes to know how your lover is being cared for by the Christians, and from hence I am going on to see our sick boy."

"Then ask your friends," the gem-cutter broke in, to keep less ferocious dogs for the future."

"That," replied the freedman, "will be unnecessary, for it is not likely that the fierce brute belongs to the community whose friendship I am proud to claim; and, if it does, they will be as much grieved over the matter as we can be."

"A Christian would never do another an ill turn!" said Heron, with a shrug.

"Never, so far as justice permits," replied Andreas, decisively. Then he inquired whether Heron had any message or news to send to his son; and when the gem-cutter replied that he had not, the freedman was about to go. Melissa, however, detained him, saying:

"I will go with you if you will allow me."

"And I?" said Heron, irritably. "It seems to me that children are learning to care less and less what their fathers' views and requirements may be. I have to go to Philip. Who knows what may happen in my absence? Besides—no offense to you, Andreas—what concern has my daughter among the Christians?"

"To visit her lover," replied Andreas, sharply. And he added, more quietly: "It will be a pleasure to me to escort her; and your Argutis is a faithful fellow, and in case of need would be of more use here than an inexperienced girl. I see no reasonable ground for detaining her, Heron. I should like afterwards to take her home with me, across the lake; it would be a comfort to Polybius and soothe his pain to have his favorite with him, his future daughter.—Get ready, my child."

The artist had listened with growing anger, and a swift surge of rage made him long to give the freedman a sharp lesson. But when his glaring eye met the Christian's steady, grave gaze, he controlled himself, and only said, with a shrug which sufficiently expressed his feeling that he was surrendering his veto against his better judgment, addressing himself to Melissa and ignoring Andreas:

"You are betrothed, and of age. Go, for aught I care, in obedience to him whose wishes evidently outweigh mine. Polybius's son is your master henceforth."

He folded his mantle, and when the girl hastened to help him he allowed her to do it; but he went on, to the freedman: "And for aught I care, you may take her across the lake, too. It is natural that Polybius should wish to see his future daughter. But one thing I may ask for myself: You have slaves and to spare; if anything happens to Alexander, let me hear of it at once."

He kissed Melissa on the head, nodded patronizingly to Andreas, and left the house.

His soft-hearted devotion to a vision had weakened his combativeness; still, he would have yielded less readily to a man who had once been a slave, but that the invitation to Melissa released him of her presence for a while.

He was not, indeed, afraid of his daughter; but she need not know that he wanted Philip to make him acquainted with Serapion, and that through his mediation he hoped at least to see the spirit of the wife he mourned. When he was fairly out of the house he smiled with satisfaction like a school-boy who had escaped his master.

CHAPTER VII.

Melissa, too, had a sense of freedom when she found herself walking by the side of Andreas.

In the garden of Hermes, where her father's house stood, there were few signs of the excitement with which the citizens awaited Caesar's arrival. Most of those who were out and about were going in the opposite direction; they meant to await the grand reception of Caracalla at the eastern end of the city, on his way from the Kanopic Gate to the Gate of the Sun. Still, a good many—men, women and children—were, like themselves, walking westward, for it was known that Caesar would alight at the Serapeum.

They had scarcely left the house when Andreas asked the girl whether she had a kerchief or a veil in the basket the slave was carrying behind her; and on her replying in the affirmative, he expressed his satisfaction; for Caracalla's soldiery, in consequence of the sovereign's weakened discipline and reckless liberality, were little better than an unbridled rabble.

"Then let us keep out of their way," urged Melissa.

"Certainly, as much as possible," said her companion. "At any rate, let us hurry, so as to get back to the lake before the crowd stops the way.

"You have passed an eventful and anxious night, my child, and are tired, no doubt."

"Oh, no!" said she, calmly; "I had some wine to refresh me, and some food with the Christians."

"Then they received you kindly?"

"The only woman there nursed Diodoros like a mother; and the men were considerate and careful. My father does not know them; and yet—Well, you know how much he dislikes them."

"He follows the multitude," returned Andreas, "the common herd, who hate everything exceptional, everything that disturbs their round of life, or startles them out of the quietude of their dull dreams. Woe to those who call by its true name what those blind souls call pleasure and enjoyment as serving to hasten the flight of time—not too long at the most; woe to those who dare raise even a finger against it!"

The man's deep, subdued tones were strongly expressive of the wrath within him; and the girl, who kept close to his side, asked with eager anxiety, "Then my father was right when he said that you are a member of the Christian body?"

"Yes," he replied, emphatically; and when Melissa curiously inquired whether it were true that the followers of the crucified God had renounced their love for home and country, which yet ought to be dear to every true man, Andreas answered with a superior smile, that even the founder of the Stoa had required not only of his fellow-Greeks but of all human beings, that they should regulate their existence by the same laws, since they were brethren in reason and sense.

"He was right," added Andreas, more earnestly, "and I tell you, child, the time is not far off when men shall no longer speak of Roman and Greek, of Egyptian and Syrian, of free men and slaves; when there shall be but one native land, but one class of life for all. Yea, the day is beginning to dawn even now. The fullness of the time is come!"

Melissa looked up at him in amazement, exclaiming: "How strange! I have heard those words once to-day already, and can not get them out of my head. Nay, when you confirmed my father's report, I made up my mind to ask you to explain them."

"What words?" asked Andreas, in surprise. "The fullness of the time is come."

"And where did you hear them?"

"In the house where Diodoros and I took refuge from Zminis."

"A Christian meeting-house," replied Andreas, and his expressive face darkened. "But those who assemble there are aliens to me; they follow evil heresies. But never mind—they also call themselves Christians, and the words which led you to ponder, stand to me at the very gate of the doctrine of our divine master, like the obelisks before the door of an Egyptian temple. Paul, the great preacher of the faith, wrote them to the Galatians. They are easy to understand; nay, any one who looks about him with his eyes open, or searches his own soul, can scarcely fail to see their meaning, if only the desire is roused in him for something better than what these cursed times can give us who live in them."

"Then it means that we are on the eve of great changes?"

"Yes!" cried Andreas, "only the word you use is too feeble. The old dull sun must set, to rise again with greater glory."

Ill at ease, and by no means convinced, Melissa looked her excited companion in the face as she replied:

"Of course I know, Andreas, that you speak figuratively, for the sun which lights the day seems to me bright enough; and is not everything flourishing in this gay, busy city? Are not its citizens under the protection of the law?

Were the gods ever more zealously worshiped? Is my father wrong when he says that it is a proud thing to belong to the mightiest realm on earth, before whose power barbarians tremble; a great thing to feel and call yourself a Roman citizen?"

So far Andreas had listened to her with composure, but he here interrupted, in a tone of scorn "Oh, yes! Caesar has made your father, and your neighbor Skopas, and every free man in the country a Roman citizen; but it is a pity that, while he gave each man his patent of citizenship, he should have filched the money out of his purse."

"Apion, the dealer, was saying something to that effect the other day, and I dare say it is true. But I can not be persuaded against the evidence of my own eyes, and they light on many good and pleasant things. If only you had been with us to the Nekropolis yesterday! Every man was honoring the gods after his own manner. Some, indeed, were grave enough; still, cheerfulness won the day among the people. Most of them were full of the god. I myself, who generally live so quietly, was infected as the mystics came back from Eleusis, and we joined their ranks."

"'Till the spy Zminis spoiled your happiness and imperiled your brother's life for a careless speech."

"Very true!"

"And what your brother heedlessly proclaimed," Andreas went on, with flashing eyes, "the very sparrows twitter on the house-tops. It is the truth. The sovereign of the Roman Empire is a thousand times a murderer. Some he sent to precede his own brother, and they were followed by all— twenty thousand, it is said—who were attached to the hapless Geta, or who even spoke his name. This is the lord and master to whom we owe obedience whom God has set over us for our sins. And when this wretch in the purple shall close his eyes, he, like the rest of the criminals who have preceded him on the throne, will be proclaimed a god! A noble company! When your beloved mother died I heard you, even you, revile the gods for their cruelty; others call them kind. It is only a question of how they accept the blood of the sacrificed beasts, their own creatures, which you shed in their honor. If Serapis does not grant some fool the thing he asks, then he turns to the altar of Isis, of Anubis, of Zeus, of Demeter. At last he cries to Sabazios, or one of the new deities of Olympus, who owe their existence to the decisions of the Roman Senate, and who are for the most part scoundrels and villains. There certainly never were more gods than there are now; and among those of whom the myths tell us things strange enough to bring those who worship them into contempt, or to the gallows, is the countless swarm of good and evil daimons. Away with your Olympians! They ought to reward virtue and punish vice; and they are no better than corruptible judges; for you know beforehand just what and how much will avail to purchase their favors."

"You paint with dark colors," the girl broke in. "I have learned from Philip that the Pythagoreans teach that not the sacrifice, but the spirit of the offering, is what really matters."

"Quite right. He was thinking, no doubt, of the miracle-monger of Tyana, Apollonius, who certainly had heard of the doctrine of the Redeemer. But among the thousand nine hundred and ninety, who here bring beasts to the altar, who ever remembers this? Quite lately I heard one of our garden laborers ask how much a day he ought to sacrifice to the sun, his god. I told him a keration—for that is what the poor creature earns for a whole day's work. He thought that too much, for he must live; so the god must be content with a tithe, for the taxes to the State on his earnings were hardly more."

"The divinity ought no doubt to be above all else to us," Melissa observed. "But when your laborer worships the sun, and looks for its benefits, what is the difference between him and you, or me, or any of us, though we call the sun Helios or Serapis, or what not?"

"Yes, yes," replied Andreas. "The sun is adored here under many different names and forms, and your Serapis has swallowed up not only Zeus and Pluto, but Phoebus Apollo and the Egyptian Osiris and Ammon, and Ra, to swell his own importance. But to be serious, child, our fathers made to themselves many gods indeed, of the sublime phenomena and powers of Nature, and worshiped them admiringly; but to us only the names remain, and those who offer to Apollo never think of the sun. With my laborer, who is an Arab, it is different. He believes the light-giving globe itself to be a god; and you, I perceive, do not think him wholly wrong. But when you see a youth throw the discus with splendid strength, do you praise the discus, or the thrower?"

"The thrower," replied Melissa. "But Phoebus Apollo himself guides his chariot with his divine hands."

"And astronomers," the Christian went on, "can calculate for years to come exactly where his steeds will be at each minute of the time. So no one can be more completely a slave than he to whom so many mortals pray that he will, of his own free-will, guide circumstances to suit them. I, therefore, regard the sun as a star, like any other star; and worship should be given, not to those rolling spheres moving across the sky in prescribed paths, but to Him who created them and guides them by fixed laws. I really pity your Apollo and the whole host of the Olympian gods, since the world has become possessed by the mad idea that the gods and daimons may be moved, or even compelled, by forms of prayer and sacrifices and magic arts, to grant to each worshiper the particular thing on which he may have set his covetous and changeable fancy."

"And yet," exclaimed Melissa, "you yourself told me that you prayed for my mother when the leech saw no further hope. Every one hopes for a miracle from the immortals when his own power has come to an end! Thousands think so. And in our city the people have never been more religious than they are now. The singer of the Ialemos at the feast of Adonis particularly praised us for it."

"Because they have never been more fervently addicted to pleasure, and therefore have never more deeply dreaded the terrors of hades. The great and splendid Zeus of the Greeks has been transformed into Serapis here, on the banks of the Nile, and has become a god of the nether world. Most of the ceremonies and mysteries to which the people crowd are connected with death. They hope that the folly over which they waste so many hours will smooth their way to the fields of the blest, and yet they themselves close the road by the pleasures they indulge in. But the fullness of time is now come; the straight road lies open to all mankind, called as they are to a higher life in a new world, and he who follows it may await death as gladly as the bride awaits the bridegroom on her marriage day. Yes, I prayed to my God for your dying mother, the sweetest and best of women. But what I asked for her was not that her life might be preserved, or that she might be permitted to linger longer among us, but that the next world might be opened to her in all its glory."

At this point the speaker was interrupted by an armed troop which thrust the crowd aside to make way for the steers which were to be slaughtered in the Temple of Serapis at the approach of Caesar. There were several hundred of them, each with a garland about its, neck, and the handsomest which led the train had its horns gilded.

When the road was clear again, Andreas pointed to the beasts, and whispered to his companion "Their blood will be shed in honor of the future god Caracalla. He once killed a hundred bears in the arena with his own hand. But I tell you, child, when the fullness of time is come, innocent blood shall no more be shed. You were speaking with enthusiasm of the splendor of the Roman Empire. But, like certain fruit-trees in our garden which we manure with blood, it has grown great on blood, on the life-juice of its victims. The mightiest realm on earth owes its power to murder and rapine; but now sudden destruction is coming on the insatiate city, and visitation for her sins."

"And if you are right—if the barbarians should indeed destroy the armies of Caesar," asked Melissa, looking up in some alarm at the enthusiast, "what then?"

"Then we may thank those who help to demolish the crumbling house!" cried Andreas, with flashing eyes.

"And if it should be so," said the girl, with tremulous anxiety, "what universal ruin! What is there on earth that could fill its place? If the empire falls into the power of the barbarians, Rome will be made desolate, and all the provinces laid waste which thrive under her protection."

"Then," said Andreas, "will the kingdom of the Spirit arise, in which peace and love shall reign instead of hatred and murder and wars. There shall be one fold and one Shepherd, and the least shall be equal with the greatest."

"Then there will be no more slaves?" asked Melissa, in growing amazement.

"Not one," replied her companion, and a gleam of inspiration seemed to light up his stern features. "All shall be free, and all united in love by the grace of Him who hath redeemed us."

But Melissa shook her head, and Andreas, understanding what was passing in her mind, tried to catch her eye as he went on:

"You think that these are the impossible wishes of one who has himself been a slave, or that it is the remembrance of past suffering and unutterable wrong which speaks in me? For what right-minded man would not desire to preserve others from the misery which once crushed him to earth with its bitter burden?—But you are mistaken. Thousands of free- born men and women think as I do, for to them, too, a higher Power has revealed that the fullness of time is now come. He, the Greatest and Best, who made all the woes of the world His own, has chosen the poor rather than the rich, the suffering rather than the happy, the babes rather than the wise and prudent; and in his kingdom the last shall be first—yea, the least of the last, the poorest of the poor; and they, child, are the slaves."

He ended his diatribe with a deep sigh, but Melissa pressed the hand which held hers as they walked along the raised pathway, and said: "Poor Andreas! How much you must have gone through before Polybius set you free!"

He only nodded, and they both remained silent till they found themselves in a quiet side street. Then the girl looked up at him inquiringly, and began again:

"And now you hope for a second Spartacus? Or will you yourself lead a rebellion of the slaves? You are the man for it, and I can be secret."

"If it has to be, why not?" he replied, and his eyes sparkled with a strange fire. But seeing that she shrank from him, a smile passed over his countenance, and he added in a soothing tone: "Do not be alarmed, my child; what must come will come, without another Spartacus, or bloodshed, or turmoil. And you, with your clear eyes and your kind heart, would you find it difficult to distinguish right from wrong, and to feel for the sorrows of others—? Yes, perhaps! For what will not custom excuse and sanctify? You can pity the bird which is shut into a cage too small for it, or the mule which breaks down under too heavy a load, and the cruelty which hurts them rouses your indignation. But for the man whom a terrible fate has robbed of his freedom, often through the fault of another, whose soul endures even greater torments than his despised body, you have no better comfort than the advice which might indeed serve a philosopher, but which to him is bitter mockery: to bear his woes with patience. He is only a slave, bought, or perhaps inherited. Which of you ever thinks of asking who gave you, who are free, the right to enslave half of all the inhabitants of the Roman Empire, and to rob them of the highest prerogative of humanity? I know that many philosophers have spoken of slavery as an injustice done by the strong to the weak: but they shrugged their shoulders over it nevertheless, and excused it as an inevitable evil; for, thought they, who will serve me if my slave is regarded as my equal? You only smile at this confusion of the meditative recluses, but you forget"—and a sinister fire glowed in his eyes—"that the slave, too, has a soul, in which the same feelings stir as in your own. You never think how a proud man may feel whose arm you brand, and whose very breath of life is indignity; or what a slave thinks who is spurned by his master's foot, though noble blood may run in his veins. All living things, even the plants in the garden, have a right to happiness, and only develop fully in freedom, and under loving care; and yet one half of mankind robs the other half of this right. The sum total of suffering and sorrow to which Fate had doomed the race is recklessly multiplied and increased by the guilt of men themselves. But the cry of the poor and wretched has gone up to heaven, and now that the fullness of time is come, 'Thus far, and no farther,' is the word. No wild revolutionary has been endowed with a giant's strength to burst the bonds of the victims asunder. No, the Creator and Preserver of the world sent his Son to redeem the poor in spirit, and, above all, the brethren and the sisters who are weary and heavy laden. The magical word which shall break the bars of the prisons where the chains of the slaves are heard is Love. . . . But you, Melissa, can but half comprehend all this," he added, interrupting the ardent flow of his enthusiastic speech. "You can not understand it all. For you, too, child, the fullness of time is coming; for you, too, freeborn though you are, are, I know, one of the heavy laden who patiently suffer the burden laid upon you. You too—But keep close to me; we shall find it difficult to get through this throng."

It was, in fact, no easy matter to get across the crowd which was pouring noisily down the street of Hermes, into which this narrow way led. How ever, they achieved it, and when Melissa had recovered her breath in a quiet lane in Rhakotis, she turned to her companion again with the question, "And when do you suppose that your predictions will be fulfilled?"

"As soon as the breeze blows which shall shake the overripe fruit from the tree. It may be tomorrow, or not yet, according to the long- suffering of the Most High. But the entire collapse of the world in which we have been living is as certain to come as that you are walking here with me!"

Melissa walked on with a quaking heart, as she heard her friend's tone of conviction; he, however, was aware that the inmost meaning of his words was sealed to her. To his inquiry, whether she could not rejoice in the coming of the glorious time in store for redeemed humanity, she answered, tremulously:

"All you hope for is glorious, no doubt, but what shall lead to it must be a terror to all. Were you told of the kingdom of which you speak by an oracle, or is it only a picture drawn by your imagination, a vision, and the offspring of your soul's desire?"

"Neither," said Andreas, decidedly; and he went on in a louder voice: "I know it by revelation. Believe me, child, it is as certainly true as that the sun will set this night. The gates of the heavenly Jerusalem stand open, and if you, too, would fain be blessed—But more of this later. Here we are at our journey's end."

They entered the Christian home, where they found Diodoros, on a comfortable couch, in a spacious, shady room, and in the care of a friendly matron.

But he was in an evil case. The surgeon thought his wound a serious one; for the heavy stone which had hit him had injured the skull, and the unhappy youth was trembling with fever. His head was burning, and it was with difficulty that he spoke a few coherent words. But his eyes betrayed that he recognized Melissa, and that it was a joy to him to see her again; and when he was told that Alexander had so far escaped, a bright look lighted up his countenance. It was evidently a comfort to him to gaze on Melissa's pretty face; her hand lay in his, and he understood her when she greeted him from her father, and spoke to him of various matters; but the lids ere long closed over his aching eyes.

Melissa felt that she must leave him to rest. She gently released his hand from her grasp and laid it across his breast, and moved no more, excepting to wipe the drops from his brow. Solemn stillness had reigned for some time in the large, clean house, faintly smelling of lavender; but, on a sudden, doors opened and shut; steps were heard in the anteroom, seats were moved, and a loud confusion of men's voices became audible, among them that of Andreas.

Melissa listened anxiously to the heated discussion which had already become a vehement quarrel. She longed to implore the excited wranglers to moderate their tones, for she could see by her lover's quivering lips that the noise hurt him; but she could not leave him.

The dispute meanwhile grew louder and louder. The names of Montanus and Tertullian, Clemens and Origen, fell on her ear, and at last she heard Andreas exclaim in high wrath: "You are like the guests at a richly furnished banquet who ask, after they have well eaten, when the meat will be brought in. Paraclete is come, and yet you look for another."

He was not allowed to proceed; fierce and scornful contradiction checked his speech, till a voice of thunder was heard above the rest:

"The heavenly Jerusalem is at hand. He who denies and doubts the calling of Montanus is worse than the heathen, and I, for one, cast him off as neither a brother nor a Christian!"

This furious denunciation was drowned in uproar; the anxious girl heard seats overturned, and the yells and shouts of furious combatants; the suffering youth meanwhile moaned with anguish, and an expression of acute pain was stamped on his handsome features. Melissa could bear it no longer; she had risen to go and entreat the men to make less noise, when suddenly all was still.

Diodoros immediately became calmer, and looked up at the girl as gratefully as though the soothing silence were owing to her. She could now hear the deep tones of the head of the Church of Alexandria, and understood that the matter in hand was the readmission into this congregation of a man who had been turned out by some other sect. Some would have him rejected, and commended him to the mercy of God; others, less rigid, were willing to receive him, since he was ready to submit to any penance.

Then the quarrel began again. High above every other voice rose the shrill tones of a man who had just arrived from Carthage, and who boasted of personal friendship with the venerable Tertullian. The listening girl could no longer follow the connection of the discussion, but the same names again met her ear; and, though she understood nothing of the matter, it annoyed her, because the turmoil disturbed her lover's rest.

It was not till the sick-nurse came back that the tumult was appeased; for, as soon as she learned how seriously the loud disputes of her fellow-believers were disturbing the sick man's rest, she interfered so effectually, that the house was as silent as before.

The deaconess Katharine was the name by which she was known, and in a few minutes she returned to her patient's bedside.

Andreas followed her, with the leech, a man of middle height, whose shrewd and well-formed head, bald but for a little hair at the sides, was set on a somewhat ungainly body. His sharp eyes looked hither and thither, and there was something jerky in his quick movements; still, their grave decisiveness made up for the lack of grace. He paid no heed to the bystanders, but threw himself forward rather than bent over the patient, felt him, and with a light hand renewed his bandages; and then he looked round the room, examining it as curiously as though he proposed to take up his abode there, ending by fixing his prominent, round eyes on Melissa. There was something so ruthlessly inquisitive in that look that it might, under other circumstances, have angered her. However, as it was, she submitted to it, for she saw that it was shrewd, and she would have called the wisest physician on earth to her lover's bedside if she had had the power.

When Ptolemaeus—for so he was called—had, in reply to the question, "who is that?" learned who she was, he hastily murmured: "Then she can do nothing but harm here. A man in a fever wants but one thing, and that is perfect quiet."

And he beckoned Andreas to the window, and asked him shortly, "Has the girl any sense?"

"Plenty," replied the freedman, decisively.

"As much, at any rate, as she can have at her age," the other retorted. "Then it is to be hoped that she will go without any leave-taking or tears. That fine lad is in a bad way. I have known all along what might do him good, but I dare not attempt it alone, and there is no one in Alexandria. . . . But Galen has come to join Caesar. If he, old as he is—But it is not for the likes of us to intrude into Caesar's quarters—Still—"

He paused, laying his hand on his brow, and rubbing it thoughtfully with his short middle finger. Then he suddenly exclaimed: "The old man would never come here. But the Serapeum, where the sick lie awaiting divine or diabolical counsel in dreams—Galen will go there. If only we could carry the boy thither."

"His nurse here would hardly allow that," said Andreas, doubtfully.

"He is a heathen." replied the leech, hotly. "Besides, what has faith to do with the injury to the body? How many Caesars have employed Egyptian and Jewish physicians? The lad would get the treatment he needs, and, Christian as I am, I would, if necessary, convey him to the Serapeum, though it is of all heathen temples the most heathen. I will find out by hook or by crook at what time Galen is to visit the cubicles. To-morrow, or next day at latest; and to-night, or, better still, to-morrow morning before sunrise, I will have the youth carried there. If the deaconess refuses—"

"And she will," Andreas put in.

"Very well.—Come here, maiden," he beckoned to Melissa, and went on loud enough for the deaconess to hear: "If we can get your betrothed to the Serapeum early to-morrow, he may probably be cured; otherwise I refuse to be responsible. Tell your friends and his that I will be here before sunrise to-morrow, and that they must provide a covered litter and good bearers."

He then turned to the deaconess, who had followed him in silence, with her hands clasped like a deserter, laid his broad, square hand on her shoulder, and added:

"So it must be, Widow Katharine, Love endures and suffers all things, and to save a neighbor's life, it is well to suffer in silence even things that displease us. I will explain it all to you afterwards. Quiet, only perfect quiet—No melancholy leave-taking, child! The sooner you are out of the house the better."

He went back again to the bed, laid his hand for a moment on the sick man's forehead, and then left the room.

Diodoros lay still and indifferent on the couch. Melissa kissed him on the brow, and withdrew without his observing it, her eyes full of tears.